# GRANNY

*SREEVINO*

**Ukiyoto Publishing**

All global publishing rights are held by

**Ukiyoto Publishing**

Published in 2023

Content Copyright © Sreevino

**ISBN 9789360168643**

*All rights reserved.*
*No part of this publication may be reproduced, transmitted, or stored in a retrieval system, in any form by any means, electronic, mechanical, photocopying, recording or otherwise, without the prior permission of the publisher.*

*The moral rights of the author have been asserted. This is a work of fiction. Names, characters, businesses, places, events, locales, and incidents are either the products of the author's imagination or used in a fictitious manner. Any resemblance to actual persons, living or dead, or actual events is purely coincidental.*

*This book is sold subject to the condition that it shall not by way of trade or otherwise, be lent, resold, hired out or otherwise circulated, without the publisher's prior consent, in any form of binding or cover other than that in which it is published.*

*This title is produced in Association with Pachyderm Tales*

**www.pachydermtales.com**

## ACKNOWLEDGEMENT

I whole heartedly thank,

Mohanasundari Jaganathan,

(Managing Director of Sharp Electrodes Pvt Ltd)

for funding this project.

Without her, this book would not be possible!

This book was a part of workshop conducted in our college, NGM College Pollachi and Pachyderm Tales.

I whole heartedly thank our management, our teachers and HOD of English Dept, NGM as well as Suja Mam for this initiative.

Thanks to my friend to support and help me to complete my work.

# Do you know who I am?

I am the little
Granddaughter of
my
lovely grandmother.

Do you want to know about her?

Let me tell you about my grandmother.

# Granny

There is this beautiful lady who would be waiting outside by 2:45 pm to receive her Granddaughter from school.

# Granny

She cooks different dishes and sweets for her granddaughter.

# Granny

She can measure the ingredients for cooking without the help of any measuring devices as she's an experienced cook for which I admire her very much.

# Granny

As I do not have many friends around me, my grandmother is my one and only best friend.

She plays with me all the time without being bored.

# Granny 11

She is 85 but her attitude and behaviour is still young like a teenager.

# Granny

Whenever my cousins fight and do not want to play with me, my grandmother will play with me. We talk about a lot of things.

# Granny

She is also my PET teacher.

I am not the type of person who spends a lot of money on buying useless things.

But I buy a lot of things to play with my grandmother. We buy things to eat more.

My parents give me very little money as I'm still a kid.
But she is my piggy bank...

You guessed it right!

Yes, my grandmother gives me money.

Not too much, but enough to buy things that make me happy.

"Aahh chooo...."

Yes, whenever I'm not feeling well, my first doctor is my grandmother.

There is no need for medicines and injections which give more pain than cure.

She identifies my problem and gives me medicine made by her own hands.

Along with being my PET teacher and piggy bank, she is also my doctor.

A lady with white hair, shivering hands, wrinkled skin, counting her last days, but she is full of love and joy... full of life.

## The Author

Sreevino. P is a B.A English Literature, final year student at NGM college, She stepped into writing for the first time and is giving her best. "Granny" is the first book of hers. She strongly believes in her love for her family and friends without any form of boundaries.

## The Illustrator

Udhayabharathi. K is doing B.Com final year. Student of NGM college. She is very much interested drawing. A budding artist and this what she does in her free time. She dreams of giving life to characters through her art work.

www.ingramcontent.com/pod-product-compliance
Lightning Source LLC
LaVergne TN
LVHW041643070526
838199LV00053B/3534